The Vixen's Bark

Paranormal Council Book 2

Laura Greenwood

Visit Laura Greenwood's website at:

www.authorlauragreenwood.co.uk

www.facebook.com/authorlauragreenwood/

Cover Design by Ammonia Book Covers

The Vixen's Bark is a work of fiction. Names, characters, places, and incidents are the products of the author's imagination or are used fictitiously. Any resemblance to actual persons, living or dead, businesses, companies, events, or locales is entirely coincidental.

For my Dad,

Chapter 13 was written for you, and all the support you've given me over the years. Even when you didn't have to.

1

Ari watched her twin sister's litter play in the garden of their suburban home. They weren't able to shift yet, but in another couple of years they would, and she definitely didn't envy Christine that. Fox shifters were mischievous by nature, and having four little ones about was sure to be hard work. Their Mum had always told them that the two of them had been a handful, even before their younger brothers had come along, ten years after them.

"You could always retire from the council and have some of your own," Chris handed her a glass of cold water, which she took gratefully. It was hot, and being in the city only seemed to make it worse.

"You sound like Mum," Ari sighed. Their Mum was desperate for her to settle down with 'a nice fox shifter' and have a litter. Something she'd been even more keen on since discovering that, if she mated, Ari would lose her position on the Shifter Council. Ari had never been sure exactly why her Mum was so against her being a Council member. Even if most shifters weren't aware of who she was, it still gave her the power to change things.

"It's not for me," she muttered, receiving a disbelieving look from Chris.

"One day, you'll meet the right fox and you'll change your mind," she said with certainty as she watched her litter with an adoring face. But all Ari could focus on was the other issue she faced when it came to her family's plan for her; they expected her to mate with another fox. Without meaning to, her mind wandered to one of her fellow Council members, but she refused to dwell on that. At least she refused to until later. The two of them had been foolish to think that they could have an affair, and now, like the fool she was, she was beginning to realise that it meant something more than just sex. Perhaps it always had. Which brought her back to the issue of her family wanting her to mate, or at least marry, another fox.

"I'm not ready for children," she said, but if she was honest with herself, that wasn't entirely true. While it wasn't something she wanted to rush into, she'd thought about it more and more recently, and in a worrying amount of detail. Chris laughed, proving that even after the two of them had gone their separate directions in life, her twin knew her better than anyone.

"I don't believe you. More than that, I think you've met someone," her sister teased and all the blood drained from Ari's face.

"Chris! I could lose my seat if a rumour like that gets out!" She glanced around reflexively, even if she knew that the two of them were alone, she couldn't help but be a little paranoid.

"That's not a no," Chris smirked at her.

"I haven't met anyone," Ari lied, forcing her thoughts away from Bjorn's kisses lest her sister work out the direction her mind was taking her. She technically wasn't lying either; it'd taken Bjorn, and the tension thrumming between them, months to wear her down and kick start their affair. An affair that she wasn't convinced she'd be able to stop even if she wanted to. He was like an addiction to her; a tall, dark and handsome addiction that did amazing things to her body.

"Mmm," Ari knew that Chris didn't believe her, but she wasn't ready to admit anything yet. Chris had inherited their Mum's sense of tradition, and that didn't pair well with Ari's bear shifter lover. "How's work?" Ari was grateful for Chris' change of subject.

"It's good, I won my case last week," she followed her sister's gaze to where the litter was playing a game of hide and seek, one that seemed to involve a lot of pouncing.

"The murder?"

"Yes, it was easy to prove the woman was innocent," particularly because one look at the case notes had told Ari that a necromancer was the true culprit. She'd alerted the Councils, and Bjorn was looking into it using his PI connections, but the real culprit had yet to be caught. "Are you coming back to work?" Chris had gone on maternity leave when she'd had the litter, and had then added on a sabbatical, but their boss was becoming more and more demanding about her coming back.

"I don't think I will. How could I leave them?" While she wasn't sure she felt the same way as her sister, she could understand. Growing up, family life had been important, and their parents had instilled the same values in their children. Some of that lived on in

Ari too, but she liked to think that she'd added some more modern values somewhere along the way. That was partly why it was so important for her to be on the Shifter Council, and why she'd become a lawyer; it made her feel as if she could make a difference.

Despite himself, Bjorn's attention focused on the door every time it opened, desperate to see Ari the moment she arrived. He knew that he probably shouldn't be so obvious in his attraction for her, especially not in the Council chambers, but he just couldn't help it. Technically, what the two of them were up to went against Council rules, and if they were discovered then they'd both lose their seats. And yet, that wasn't enough to make him want to stop, especially since Ari had revealed the truth behind mating. He'd been labouring under the illusion that mating required a bite, but apparently, it didn't work like that. All true mates needed to do was meet, and since learning that, barely a moment had passed when he hadn't thought of Ari; the truth that he'd thought he knew fast becoming something he was sure about.

"Sorry I'm late," her lilting voice broke through his thoughts and he had to stop the grin spreading across his face. Everyone knew him as the gruff bear shifter who was too jaded to smile at anyone, and he couldn't go about ruining that reputation, even if he had felt himself softening to the outside world more recently. To his surprise, Ari threw him a small smile as she sat in the only empty Council seat, the other three having arrived shortly after he had.

"Anything wrong?" Nathalie asked from her seat next to Bjorn. He was surprised to see her wearing a powder blue suit rather than the white dresses that she normally preferred. He'd never really understood why unicorns were so focused on the colour white, but they all seemed to be, and for Nathalie to be wearing any colour at all was odd. Her skin shimmered in the dim light of the Council chamber, but Bjorn had long since stopped noticing her ethereal beauty, which paled in comparison to the auburn-haired vixen sat a few seats down.

"Court ran over," Ari waved a hand dismissively, though Bjorn could tell from the tight set of her mouth that there was something more going on. If he was lucky, he might have a chance to get it out of her later. "But more importantly, how are we coming on with the necromancer problem?" Their eyes met as she looked at him, not a hidden look this time, as this was an issue that the other Council members knew they were working on together.

"No name yet," he responded briefly.

"I have a meeting with a necromancer representative tomorrow," Alden added. He was sat between Nathalie and Ari, and often stayed quiet unless he felt he had something valuable to add. Bjorn liked that about the guy, he didn't have time to suffer fools.

"Just a representative?" Ari responded, her smile slipping slightly, revealing to Bjorn how down cast the whole situation was making her. While working on her previous case, she'd noticed that the murder victim showed all the signs of being targeted by a necromancer, and she'd instantly told the Councils about it. He'd then had to watch as she worked herself to the bone to get the accused woman acquitted of the charge, showing a rare determination that not many had. It was one of the many reasons he liked her so much.

"You know what they're like Ari," Bjorn interrupted before Alden could reply, only to receive a death glare for using her nickname. He cursed inwardly, not knowing how it had slipped out. They were normally so careful about keeping their relationship under wraps and not raising suspicion. Which was often difficult, especially considering how little he knew about the other Council members in comparison to how much he knew about Ari. He wasn't sure how it'd got to this point, but like everything else between them, it had just clicked into place.

"Can we use the nymph support to force them to be more cooperative?" Nathalie asked softly.

"Are we sure that we want to call on them so soon?" Alden countered. A hissing laugh came from the seat next to Bjorn.

"So, we make a big deal about marrying that panther to a nymph and you don't want to use that! Typical bird. I thought you were supposed to be wise?" Drayce bit out. Bjorn had always wondered why he was on the Council, particularly when he seemed so uninterested most of the time. Alden's head swivelled round to look Drayce in the eye, and the two stared off, neither of them saying a word.

"Boys!" Ari interrupted, clicking her fingers and breaking the staring contest. Beside him, Nathalie sighed. As much as he hated it, this was often how the meetings went. Drayce seemed to hate everyone and it riled the normally calm Alden up the wrong way. "We can at least ask Aella if they'd support us, I know she's trying to get the High Council to introduce stricter rules around blood slaves, so she might have something for us on that front."

"Unfortunately, there doesn't seem to be any way of telling who even is a necromancer, they keep their records even more under wraps than we do," even as he spoke, Bjorn found himself getting annoyed at them. They were worse than vampires as far as he was concerned. Sure, there were vampires that went off the rails, but their Council liked to make a big song and dance about punishing them. On the other hand, the Necromancer Council seemed to stop just short of encouraging their people to kill so they could practice their art. It was all very shady.

They moved on from the Necromancer issue, and Bjorn was grateful that there didn't seem to be too much going on in the shifter world, other than a disagreeable divorce relating to a false mating; a cautionary tale to any shifters attempting a relationship with each other. He'd glanced towards Ari while they were talking, but she was studiously avoiding his gaze.

3

She watched as the other three left the Council chambers, packing away her own things slowly in the hope that she could snatch a few private moments with Bjorn. If she felt like being sensible, then she knew that the two of them really needed to talk about what they were doing. It was dangerous, and could lead to them both of them losing their positions, as well as risking a false mating. And yet, there was a part of her that wasn't willing to stop.

A firm but gentle hand gripped her elbow and spun her around, lifting her by the waist so that she was sat on one of the desks. Bjorn stepped so that he as standing between her legs and brought his lips to hers without saying a word. The pent-up desire between them took hold and came through their kiss, causing whimpers to come from Ari as her teeth lengthened. She pulled away from his kiss before she did something stupid like nip his lip and draw blood. Doing that, even without meaning to, would bind them together in a way that she wasn't ready for. But that didn't stop Bjorn. He feathered kisses down her neck and she leaned back, allowing him access and arching her back more, causing Bjorn's bucking hips to press in close to where she wanted him most. Her hands tugged at his shirt and he stepped back, whipping it over his head and throwing it to the floor. His jeans quickly followed suit. Ari took a moment to appreciate the view, before ridding herself of her own clothes and perching back on the desk completely naked; she knew it was wrong, but being in the Council chambers only added to her excitement. Just like it had the other times.

Bjorn stalked towards her, a predatory glint in his eye, sending shivers down Ari's spine. They'd tried to stop more than once during the six months or so they'd been sleeping together. It hadn't worked. Their record for staying away was a week, and that was only because Bjorn had been away with his PI work. It was a week that she didn't want to repeat ever again. She pushed the thought away, not liking what it meant for their relationship, or for her Council seat.

"I want you," Bjorn growled, stepping back between her legs, the heat he was throwing off warming her. He kissed her again and Ari was too desperate to do anything but guide him into her. Bjorn groaned deeply, and she let out an involuntary moan, revelling in the sensation of being with him. It took mere moments for the tension to begin to mount within her, building more and more as he thrust into her, his muscles flexing under her greedy hands. Bjorn trailed kisses down her throat again and he began to nip gently on her skin, making her blood sing with pleasure. Her nails scraped across his back, but she couldn't bring herself to worry about whether she was leaving any marks, and from Bjorn's grunts and moans, he didn't mind either.

The sensation of lengthening teeth against the sensitive skin of her throat broke through the pleasure surrounding them, and she hastily pushed him away.

"Bjorn! BJORN!" She tried desperately to bring him out of the haze he was in, but nothing seemed to work. His eyes were blazing with lust as he looked over her. Nothing could hide his lengthened teeth as his inner-bear come through.

After a few moments of staring, Bjorn came back to himself and a look of horror crossed his face. Ari shivered, suddenly feeling cold in the empty Council room. Bjorn handed her his shirt, which she hastily put on, buttoning it as he pulled on his jeans.

"I guess we need to talk," she could see the reluctance in the set of his jaw, but was impressed that he'd admitted it. In her experience, men never wanted to talk about relationship stuff. There was no denying that it wasn't just sex between them anymore, she had her doubts about whether it ever really had been. But Ari had also been ignoring that thought, hoping that some solution would present itself in time. Or that she'd suddenly stop thinking about the sexy bear shifter in front of her.

"I guess we do," she admitted. She'd rather be in the courtroom than deal with anything like the feelings swirling around inside her, but it was too late for that now. "You just tried to bite me."

"I know, I'm sorry." Her heart sank, as much as she had tried to tell herself that his was the reaction she wanted, she was lying to herself and knew it.

"We can't risk mating Bjorn," he looked at her oddly, as if he wanted to contradict her, but she wasn't about to let him. "We'd both lose our positions on the Council, not to mention our standing in society if we revealed we'd falsely mated. Plus, there's my family..." she trailed off, looking at the floor and not wanting to elaborate. Ari wasn't normally afraid of saying what she thought, and considering she was a lawyer, she didn't have the option to be; yet there was something about this situation that was making her nervous.

"Your family?" He raised an eyebrow, a confused look in his eyes as he waited for her to elaborate.

"Never mind that; our positions, Bjorn. We could lose them." To her surprise, Bjorn cupped her face in his hands and their eyes met.

"I would give up my position for you, Ari." There was a sincerity in his dark eyes that scared her. Almost as if he was telling her the truth; and she didn't know whether the possibility of him lying to her, or that of him telling the truth, scared her more.

"I'm…"

"Not ready for that. I know, but the minute you are, is the moment you're mine."

A thrill went through her, even if she wasn't ready to accept that there was more between them. He kissed her chastely once, and left quickly. Almost as if he was worried about what he'd do if he stayed. He was still shirtless, the marks from her fingernails giving her inner-fox a deep sense of satisfaction, almost like the vixen had marked her territory.

The real problem was that it felt like a part of Ari left with him.

4

It had been four days, three hours and six minutes since he'd last seen Ari, and it was killing him. He loved her, and wouldn't even try to deny it, not when he'd known it for a while. More than that, everything he'd told her was true; he would willingly give up his position on the Council for her. He'd willingly give up anything for her. The only reason he'd applied for a seat on the Council in the first place was so that he had somewhere to belong to. His family were all gone, victims of Russian hunters who were after their pelts, and for years, he'd had no one.

Until he'd met Ari. Despite promising himself he'd never let anyone in again, and so avoid the risk of losing them, Ari had quickly wormed her way into his future plans; even if she didn't know that yet. As far as Bjorn could tell, the main thing standing in his way was Ari's desire to make a difference, and her way of doing that was being on the Council. He wasn't about to make her give up her seat for him, and that had made him determined to find another way.

A knock sounded at the door, bringing him to his senses, and he looked up to find Kemnebi Davis stood in the doorway. The panther shifter was dressed in a formal suit, with a five o'clock shadow on his jaw. While Kem was a big man himself, he was shorter and not quite as broad as Bjorn, not that that would make him any less intimidating to anyone that wasn't like them.

"Penny for your thoughts?" Kem dropped into the chair on the other side of Bjorn's desk, relaxing back into his seat. Bjorn gave a quick envious glance at the glinting gold ring on Kem's left hand before snapping himself out of it. While the two of them hadn't been on the friendliest of terms before Kem had married and mated, he was one of the only people that knew about Bjorn's relationship with Ari, even if he had found out accidentally. And so, when he'd needed advice, he'd bitten the bullet and called him.

"I need to find a way for a mated shifter to stay on the Council," Bjorn shrugged. Kem had proved himself trustworthy enough in the past two months, and as much as he could, Bjorn had started to see him as a kind of friend.

"Ah, Arabella." He said, a knowing glint in his eye, "you don't want to give up your seat for her?" He seemed genuinely confused and Bjorn didn't blame him, not after everything Kem had been through to get his mate. That had included standing up to the Council, and considering that Ari was a force to be reckoned with, as well as the intimidation factor he and Drayce brought, it said something that Kem would go that far. For the most part, shifter society worked on earning respect, an ingrained habit from their more primitive days, and Kem had earned Bjorn's the moment he'd refused to marry Aella Dentro.

"Of course I would!" He said indignantly and watched the smirk form on Kem's face. Bjorn let out a warning growl, but Kem just chuckled.

"So you want a way to claim her and let you both keep your

seats?" Bjorn nodded, "you know, I never did understand that rule."

"It was to make sure the Council members stayed impartial," Kem laughed loudly and Bjorn had to smile in response.

"So basically, they didn't want the Council run by women."

"Pretty much."

"Despite the fact that it's now very effectively run by a woman," Bjorn was about to protest, but the look on Kem's face told him not to bother. While on the surface, the Council was an impartial group of five shifters, each with an equal amount of power, there was little doubt that it was Ari that ran the show. Pride welled up inside him at the thought of how strong a mate he was getting, even if she wasn't completely his yet.

"Despite that."

"I can talk to Aella, or get Lia to, see if they can put something to the High Council."

"Would they get involved?" Kem shrugged.

"I've no idea, but if anyone is capable of changing the system it's my sister-in-law," the smile he gave was somewhat affectionate, much to Bjorn's surprise. From what he'd heard, Kem and Aella hadn't got off to the best start. Of course, that could have been down to the fact that Kem had shown no interest in her, despite her almost infamous beauty and power. But he was now married to Aella's younger sister,

Lia, and as she was also a nymph, the link between the two Councils had happened just the way they'd wanted it to. With the added bonus of being sealed by true mates.

"I don't doubt that." Kem stood up and made for the door, but turned back around to face Bjorn before leaving.

"Does Arabella know what you're doing for her?"

"No," he admitted, thinking back to the moment in the Council chambers when he'd very nearly claimed her. Except that, ever since Ari had revealed to Kem that the biting part of mating wasn't actually necessary, he suspected that he already had, and she was just fighting the truth. His only consolation was that she wasn't fighting it because of how she felt, but rather because of what being mated would cost her.

"Maybe you should tell her how you feel," he pulled a face and Kem smiled back sadly. "Think about it Bjorn. Not telling her could end badly," he looked lost in thought, as if remembering some unpleasant experience. Kem waved goodbye, leaving Bjorn alone in his office.

"Maybe," he muttered.

5

Ari sighed as she filed away her paperwork, glad that the day was nearly over. She loved her job, especially when she managed to save innocent people from being punished for something they hadn't done. But she just hadn't been able to concentrate since the moment she'd pushed Bjorn away.

The memory kept playing through her head on repeat. Leaving her to wonder whether she should have just let him claim her. There was more than a small part of her that wanted him to, but she wasn't quite ready to give up her Council seat yet. Maybe she would be when the necromancer problem was solved, that would at least give herself a sense of closure. But then there was her family. Her sister would be happy for her, and her brothers wouldn't care, but she couldn't imagine her parents approving of a mate that wasn't a fox shifter. Well, her Dad would probably come around, but her Mum was another story.

And yet, the thought that shifters only got one true mate just wouldn't leave her head. Sure, they could falsely mate, but that just wasn't the same. That thought always seemed to be followed by a sense of certainty that Bjorn was the one for her.

Her back stiffened as she felt eyes on her, and she turned slowly, knowing who she was about to see. He looked awful, his dark hair standing on end, and his eyes drinking her in as if he was dying of thirst.

"Bjorn…you shouldn't be here," even if there was a part of her that was thrilled he was.

"Ari please, I needed to see you."

"We can't be seen together! Imagine what would happen if we were," inwardly, she begged for him to say that he didn't care, that she was more important than his reputation. Despite it all, her heart sunk slightly when he didn't.

"I found something about the necromancer," disappointment welled up inside her now that she knew he wasn't actually here for her, but she pushed it aside and tried to focus on his news.

"What?" She hated being so curt, but it was either that or cry.

"Male, about 6'3", late twenties to early thirties, dark hair," he read from a small leather bound notebook, which she knew he always kept to hand. He'd once let it slip that it was a habit he'd picked up from his father, but when she'd tried to find out more, he'd closed off. She'd let it drop after that, already worried about the way her feelings were taking her.

"So, he could be anyone then." Bjorn folded his arms across his chest, no emotion showing in his eyes. She shivered, not liking this side of him. Especially as she hadn't seen it since they first met.

"Hardly, there aren't that many necromancers," he had a point. Shifters weren't that numerous, and necromancers were even less so. Or at least, as far as the rest of the paranormal world knew they weren't. The necromancers were incredibly secretive, not sharing any information about themselves with the other Councils, even when they should. It meant that no one had any idea just how many of them existed, or how powerful, the necromancers actually were.

"Thank you, I'll send a message to Alden in the morning." He was the one with the link to the necromancers, even if it was only a tenuous one. They stood there in silence, sizing each other up and both avoiding what they truly wanted to say. "Was there anything else?" She hated sounding so disinterested, but there was little else she could do to hold it together.

"Ari…"

"I have work to do Bjorn," she turned away, but could still sense him behind her. He stepped forward, his footsteps not quite quiet enough for her enhanced hearing to miss. She could feel his hands hovering over her arms and silently begged him to touch her, even as she hated herself for being so weak. He sighed loudly and left, leaving Ari to choke back tears.

6

Bjorn didn't often feel nervous, but right now, faced with the dark-haired storm nymph he'd heard so much about, he couldn't help it. It wasn't that Aella Dentro was physically imposing; while she was tall, she was also slim, with long brown hair and a heart shaped face. After all, he was taller, and broader with a lot more physical strength. It wasn't her almost infamous temper either. No, what was making Bjorn nervous was the amount of influence this one woman had on his future with Ari.

Bjorn didn't think that he'd ever felt as bad as he had when he'd left Ari's office. He knew that she was pushing him away to try and avoid what was brewing between them, but it still hurt. And so, when he'd seen Kem's text saying that Aella was willing to try and change the laws about mated shifters, he'd been filled with relief mixed with a nervous apprehension. Apparently, she was on a mission to bring the Councils into the modern age, and changing this rule fit right into her plan. Aella flopped down into the seat on the other side of the table in the independent coffee shop, that she'd suggested meeting in. It was somewhere they weren't likely to be seen together and could easily avoid the questions that would come if anyone knew they'd met up.

"So, you want to change the rules?" She smirked at him, and Bjorn shuffled uncomfortably in his chair. He wasn't sure exactly what it was about her that had him on edge, maybe it was just the air of confidence she had about her, but there was definitely something.

"Yes," he replied in a clipped tone. She smiled more easily at him this time.

"I won't bite Bjorn…not unless I'm bitten first," she winked, making him think that she knew about shifter mating practices. Not that it was really a secret. Most of the paranormal world, and some of the human one, knew that shifters bit their mates. On top of that, Aella's younger sister was mated to Kem, and there was no way that Aella didn't know the truth.

"Yes, I want to change the rules."

"Why?" She cocked her head to the side, which he was sure most men found cute, but was coming across as more annoying to him. Aella wasn't a stupid woman, she couldn't be; she'd been a member of the Nymph Council since her father had resigned after the failed marriage pact. He didn't know what her day job was, but he assumed that it was just as demanding. People with no drive and ambition just didn't end up on the Councils. Unless they were like him, and desperate to find a purpose in life.

"Because they're outdated."

"I can't say I'd have ever pegged you as the kind to campaign for equality." Her demeanour straightened, and the coy look left her eyes, letting more of the woman she really was out. Bjorn was secretly relieved that there really was more to her than she'd let on, while simultaneously being slightly annoyed that she felt the need to pretend to be an air head around him.

"Why would it be about equality? There's nothing unequal about mated shifters not being able to sit on the Council," or at least, he didn't think there was. It was outdated certainly, and stemmed from a time when shifters didn't often mate outside their own kind, but it wasn't unequal. Aella looked at him, a confused expression on her face.

"You don't know, do you?"

"Don't know what?" He growled, and to his surprise, she didn't even flinch.

"Mated shifters can sit on the Council. If they're male." He sat there in silence as her words sunk in. Women had rarely sat on the Council until recently, so it seemed odd that that would be the rule. Plus, why wouldn't they know if that was the case? Not that it actually changed anything, not as far as Bjorn was concerned. He couldn't care less for his own seat, it was Ari's he wanted to save. "I take it you didn't know?" She asked softly and took a sip out of the coffee that must have arrived while he'd been thinking.

"How do you?" He deflected quickly, though he genuinely wanted to know. He'd asked Kem for Aella's help because she had a lot of power, and was quickly amassing more. She made sure that she knew the right people in the right places, and rumour had it that she had her eyes set on a seat on the High Council; whether she could manage it was another matter. No one, not even the member of the lower Councils, knew exactly who held seats.

"You realise there's a room dedicated to paranormal law in the Council building, right?" No, he hadn't. More than that, he was certain that none of the Shifter Council had. Otherwise, Ari would have been in that room in a flash, devouring everything she could find and learning how to apply it. There was even a chance that somewhere in that room was something that could help with the necromancer problem. He made a mental note to mention it to her. If she ever spoke to him again.

"Where?"

"Third floor, behind the fountain," he nodded, knowing where she meant but still not recalling ever being told about what was in that room.

"None of our Council knew."

"Huh," she leaned back in her chair and looked thoughtful for a moment, "so from your reaction, it's safe to say that it's not your seat you're worried about losing?"

"That's not what I said," he bit out. Too quickly it seemed, as a knowing look crossed over Aella's face.

"You didn't need to. So, who is it, Arabella or Nathalie?"

"What?" He asked, taken off guard by the fact she'd even known what question to ask.

"Look, there are only two women on the Shifter Council, Arabella

Reed and Nathalie Richards. Then there's you, asking Kem to talk to me about changing the rule about mated shifters. It doesn't take a genius to work it out." She gave him a stern look.

"It doesn't matter why I want it changed," he growled at her and Aella's eyes flashed with anger.

"You don't scare me Bjorn," he breathed in slowly, not because he was intimidated by her, but more because what he was here for was too important to throw away.

"Fine, I want it changed so a woman will agree to mate me," he acknowledged through gritted teeth and a satisfied smile moved over Aella's face.

"I'm going to assume it's Arabella, but you don't need to confirm that. Nathalie doesn't seem like your type." It almost scared him how easily this woman seemed to read him, but if it got him what he wanted then he didn't really care. Bjorn waited for Aella to speak again, knowing that whatever she said next would make or break all his plans, "it should be doable."

"Really?" He almost sighed with relief, but reminded himself that there was still a long way to go; and that was before it even came to convincing Ari to agree to them mating. Aella nodded and began to explain her plan to him. If she was to be believed, then the rules could be changed in a matter of weeks. And he did believe her. It was difficult not to. He'd not met Aella before, and the things he'd heard about her hadn't prepared him for the strength of conviction and determination that she gave off. If anyone could do it, he reckoned that Aella Dentro could.

7

Her eyes flicked over to Bjorn's empty chair without her even wanting them to. She didn't know where he was, or what he'd been doing for the past two weeks; he'd been at all the other Council meetings, just not this one. Ari told herself that she really shouldn't care, but being apart from him was starting to take its toll, in more ways that she truly cared to consider. And even if she was struggling to accept how much it was affecting her, it was difficult to ignore her irritability.

"Alden, have you had any progress?" She asked with a sigh. Every time she brought up the necromancer problem, he just waved it off as something he was working on. She almost wished that she'd taken it on herself, but her case load at work was already stacking up, she didn't need to add to that. There'd seemed to be a lot of falsely accused humans in the past few weeks, and she suspected that several of them were probably linked to the same necromancer that they were investigating. Unfortunately, she'd been focusing on her failing relationship more than on her work, leaving her further behind than she wanted to be.

"I'm working on it," Alden mumbled, an annoyed look crossing his face. Ari wondered what was going on, Alden was normally laidback, happy to watch everyone else with his large amber eyes. But like Ari, his mood seemed to have deteriorated over the past week or so.

"Not fast enough," a low rumble came from Ari's throat and took her by surprise. She'd realised that her inner-fox wasn't as calm as normal, a lack of sex would do that to any shifter, but she hadn't realised that it was quite as close to the surface as it actually was.

"I'm working on it Arabella," Alden's eyes flared with anger and the two of them stared off, not breaking apart until the doors to the Council chambers slammed open. The two of them whipped around to find out what was happening. Ari had almost forgotten about Nathalie and Drayce, but the two of them looked on too; the former with an amused smile on her face, while the latter had his usual look of disdain. Ari stared in shock as she saw Bjorn stride through the door, a wide grin on his face.

"Evening," there was a lilt to his voice that told her he was in a good mood. Possibly in a better mood than she'd ever seen him before. Her fox rose even closer to the surface as she realised that he was happier without her, and she had to fight to control the urge to shift and attack. Logically she knew that he'd be several times her size while shifted, and that attacking was a completely lost cause, but her fox wasn't listening to reason right at that moment in time.

"You're late," she snapped and was rewarded with a low chuckle that sent shivers down her spine.

"I had a meeting with the High Council." He looked straight at her, his dark eyes blazing with something she didn't want to risk naming for fear of being wrong, "I've brought a decree," his eyes didn't stray from Ari as he handed the decree to Nathalie. She wanted to break eye contact, to at least give them a chance to deny what was going on between them, but it had been too long since she'd seen him and her eyes refused to be torn away. Nathalie gave a short laugh, before clearing her throat. Even then, Ari didn't look away from Bjorn.

"The High Council has decreed that as of today, Council members can retain their seats once mated," Bjorn smiled at Ari, and she was sure that he was watching her as the news sunk in.

"I've got a meeting to go to," Alden muttered, rising from his seat and pushing past Bjorn. The other two following suit. She was somewhat surprised that Drayce went along with Alden and Nathalie so easily, but then again, Drayce hardly ever did what anyone expected him to.

"Wait," Bjorn held up his hand, but didn't look at them, "one more thing. As of today, I'm resigning from the Council."

"Why?" Ari blurted out before she could stop herself.

"The High Council agreed to change the rules about mated shifters, but they stipulated that a mated pair couldn't both hold seats," his gaze bore into her and she barely noticed the knowing smile on Nathalie's face.

"I accept your resignation," Alden said, "but I really have to go now."

"Have fun!" Nathalie added, following him through the door with

Drayce close behind.

"Bjorn…" tears welled in the corners of Ari's eyes as she realised that he was the one that had made this happen. While she'd been refusing to see him, he'd been working towards a future for them. A future that she'd been fighting with her insistence on siting on the Council.

"Shh, it's alright," he stepped forward and stroked a rough finger down her cheek. Surprising them both, the tears began to fall and Ari burst into huge ugly sobs.

8

Bjorn stood in front of Ari in complete shock, before snapping into action and pulling her into his arms. He didn't think he'd ever seen her cry before. Hell, he didn't think anyone had seen Ari cry, at least not since she'd been a child.

"Ari?" He asked tentatively, not wanting to upset her anymore if he could help it.

"Sorry," she sniffed and lifted one hand to his cheek, returning his earlier touch.

"There's no need to be sorry, love," he brushed a soft kiss on the top of her head and she snuggled into his chest, a warm feeling spread through him. As much as he'd wanted them to, the two of them had never had a chance to be close like this. There'd always been an air of caution between them, making sure that they weren't caught in a compromising position.

"I don't know why I'm crying," she sobbed, grabbing a handful of his shirt as she did. Bjorn tightened his arms around her. He'd hoped that his announcement would end with Ari in his arms, but not in tears.

"Probably because you're stuck with me now," he tried to joke, but the shocked look on Ari's face told him that he'd missed the mark.

"Don't ever say that," a serious look overtook her and her pale eyes met his, "I want you Bjorn."

"Good," he grunted, smoothing back a stray lock of her auburn hair.

"I love you," despite her whisper, the words sounded loud and clear around the room. They were bound to, considering he'd waited six months to hear them.

"I love you too," the tears had dried and a smile crept over her face as he closed the tiny gap between them. Their mouths touched and sparks flew, as they tended to whenever they were together. Bjorn gently pushed Ari to the floor, neither of them caring that they were in the middle of the Council chamber, or that the floor was cold; not when it was about to be one of their most important nights of their lives. "I'm going to claim you Arabella," he growled and his teeth lengthened in his mouth, an almost involuntary reaction to being near her. It was testament to his previous control that he'd only nearly claimed her once before; there was no chance of controlling himself now.

"Not if I claim you first," fire burned in her eyes and any trace of the emotional woman of just moments ago was burned away by lust. In a surprising feat of strength, along with Bjorn's cooperation, she switched their position so that his back was lying on the hard floor with her straddling him. In one swift motion, she had her shirt off; the sight of her in only a black lace bra and with her skirt pushed up to her hips, made Bjorn breathless.

Bjorn ran his hands up the outside of her legs, enjoying the small whimpering sounds she was making. She leaned down and kissed him, being careful of his lengthened teeth. Her hands moved swiftly over the buttons of his shirt, baring his chest to her. She trailed her hands over his naked skin, sending spikes of pleasure through him and causing him to thrust up to meet her; despite the fact they were both still wearing clothes.

"Ari," he grunted as she nipped along his neck. He felt her smile against his skin and flipped the two of them over once more. "Bite me," he added through shallow breathes.

"You too," she panted back, and he chuckled. He wasn't sure that he could bite her at the same time, it would probably involve a little more flexibility than he had. Seconds later, he felt her teeth sink into his skin as she claimed him. Except that she hadn't really needed to; they'd started the claim the moment they'd met, this only confirmed the bond they'd both already known was in place; even if it had taken them a while to accept it. Ari pulled back, a satisfied grin on her face.

Bjorn smiled down at her, before repeating the process, and sinking his teeth into the flesh at the base of her throat. He felt her hands on his fly, but knew that he wouldn't last. Even if that was the case, nothing could ruin this moment for him. Ari was his, and now everyone would know it.

9

Ari smiled to herself, but didn't open her eyes. The unfamiliar weight and warmth of another body in her bed being a welcome change. Bjorn had one arm wrapped tightly around her waist, pressing her body back into him and making it impossible to ignore the effect she was having on him. Feeling particularly mischievous, she nestled back further into him, and Bjorn growled low in her ear, nipping gently.

"Don't tease, Ari," she twisted her neck around so she could kiss him, and Bjorn's hand moved to cup her cheek. She still wanted him with the same burning passion she always had, but without the risk of being discovered, both of them were taking their time and getting to know each other's bodies in a way that they'd never been able to before.

"You love the tease," she whispered against his lips as they pulled apart slightly. Ari shifted on the bed so that the two of them were facing each other.

"I love you," he whispered back, grinning at her in a way that brightened his face. She already knew that he was nothing like the gruff and terse exterior he often put on for other people, but she definitely liked seeing this side of him more. Ari smiled back. Up until the night before, they'd never said the words to each other, and hearing them now made her heart leap with joy. She liked to think that they'd been on the tip of his tongue as much as they'd been on the tip of hers in the past six months.

"You better," she kissed him again, twining her arms around his neck. The next thing she knew, he'd rolled onto his back, pulling her on top of him.

An alarm blared and the two of them broke apart, both groaning in frustration. It had to happen the moment they got to the good bit. Ari rolled off him and grabbed her phone from her bedside table, shocked to see what time it actually was.

She jumped out of bed, and raced to the bathroom, leaving a confused Bjorn lying on the bed, watching her. "Come back to bed, Ari," he called out just as she stepped into the shower. The hot water hit her skin, and she felt a pang of loss as she realised she'd have to go about her day no longer smelling of Bjorn.

"I can't, I need to be in Court in an hour," she called back to him, assuming that his more acute hearing would be able to make her words out over the sound of the water.

"Call in sick," he sounded closer and she turned around to see him standing at the door of her bathroom, his eyes raking up and down her body, making her blood sizzle. Feeling particularly bold, she ran her hands down herself, palming her breasts and watching Bjorn's face as she did. His dark eyes were fixed on what she was doing, and he licked his lips, making Ari bite her lip.

"I can't," she muttered, not entirely aware of what she was doing as she slipped one of her hands between her legs. Bjorn looked as if he wanted to come barging into the shower with her, but he restrained himself, taking her by surprise by palming himself in his hand and stroking softly as he watched her.

Ari moved her hand faster, the hot water still beating down on her. Yet her blood pumped even hotter as she watched Bjorn, her breathing quickening. An explosion of pleasure tore through her and she cried out, dimly aware of Bjorn's matching sounds from outside the shower stall. She collapsed back against the wall, unable to move until large hands gently helped to rinse off her hair. She leaned back into him, enjoying the closeness.

"Will I see you tonight at least?" He spoke low in her ear, making her wish that she could do what he suggested and call in sick for the day, but her job was too important for that.

"I have to go to Mum and Dad's tonight," he spun her around but she refused to meet his gaze, worried about what he might find there.

"Can I not come with you?" His words were tentative, as if he knew that he was treading on thin ice. But surely there was no way for him to know that really. They'd talked about her family in passing, but never anything more than that. She hadn't wanted to rub in the fact that she had a family. Plus, they'd had limited time together and more important things to do with what they'd had.

"Bjorn…" she looked up, her eyes meeting his and seeing the disappointment in them. "I'm sorry, but not yet," she lifted a hand and pressed it to his cheek. Pushing up on her tiptoes, she pressed a kiss on his lips, thankful when he returned it, even if she could sense his hesitation.

"Okay," he accepted finally, but there was still part of her that suspected he wasn't happy about it. The worry lingered even after she'd arrived in Court, and didn't leave for the rest of the day.

10

"I've got a name," Bjorn kicked his feet up and rested them on Alden's desk, his size meaning that he wasn't comfortable in the other man's poky office. The whole space screamed Alden, from the crammed bookshelves that didn't seem to have any kind of system to them, to the desk covered in papers. The man himself sat on the other side of the desk, eyeing Bjorn's feet disapprovingly from behind his black framed glasses.

"Hi Bjorn, come in and take a seat," he deadpanned, taking off his glasses and pushing a hand through his sandy coloured hair, and sighed. "The name of the necromancer responsible I take it?" He leaned back in his chair, giving off a surprisingly laid back look for someone who was wearing a formal shirt and tie. Bjorn imagined that he was the Professor that all the female students talked about. He was a tall man, though he had nothing on Bjorn's height, with the lean but athletic physique which was common with bird shifters.

"Yes, he goes by Dean Winters," Bjorn handed him the sheet of paper he'd brought with him, that had everything he'd discovered about Dean on it. Unfortunately for them both, that was very little, apart from his name and a basic description. That hadn't surprised Bjorn. They were a secretive group at the best of times, even more so if they were actually doing something wrong, and Dean was the perfect example of that.

"I'll talk to Rory about it," Alden took the sheet from Bjorn's outstretched hand and studied it, pulling a face at how little information was on it. Part of Bjorn wanted to ask Alden who Rory was, but he guessed from the look on the other man's face that it was probably wasn't the right thing to say. In all likelihood, she'd just be the necromancer who'd reluctantly been assigned to work with him on the case. "So, how's Arabella this morning?" Alden raised his eyebrow and smirked.

"How would I know?" Bjorn attempted to deflect his curiosity, but knew he'd failed.

"We all know Bjorn," Alden leaned back forward, looking Bjorn straight in the eye, a risky thing to do with a bear shifter at the best of times, never mind when trying to uncover said bear shifter's secrets.

"Know what?"

"About you and Arabella." His heart sank, but he quickly reminded himself that if they'd really known, then the two of them would have been off the Council already. "We've known for months that the two of you were…dating," his tone sounded almost teasing, surprising Bjorn. While he didn't dislike Alden, he was too easy a person to get on with for that, he hadn't considered that they knew each other well enough for this kind of tease.

"Why didn't you say anything?" He asked softly, almost dreading what the other man would say.

"Well, you know Nathalie, she's a hopeless romantic really. And Drayce couldn't care less. As for me, well let's just say your mate is

39

one scary woman. I wouldn't want to get on her bad side." He laughed good naturedly, making Bjorn think that he actually held Ari in high regard, "plus, it's always been clear how much being on the Council meant to her, she takes it so seriously. You, on the other hand…well I wasn't surprised that you were the one who resigned."

"She didn't force me into it," he defended quickly.

"Never thought she did. Your reasons for being on the Council were different from the reasons the rest of us are. Even not knowing exactly what those reasons were, I could tell that much."

"Am I really that transparent?" He tried to joke, but inwardly he worried that it was true. He hoped not, or else he'd never be able to make it last with Ari. Not if she could see right through him.

"I'm just very observant." He looked at Bjorn with his unnaturally large eyes, unnerving him slightly.

"Thank you for your time, Alden, I need to get back to work," while technically true, Bjorn worked for himself, so could get away without leaving right this second. But the whole conversation had left him feeling decidedly unsettled, and he had a feeling that it was something to do with the bear in him not being sure what to make of the bird in Alden. He wasn't quite prey, but neither was he a threat. He rose from his seat and made his way from the door.

"Let me know if you find anything else, Bjorn." Alden chuckled to himself as Bjorn left. It was only once he had that he realised he hadn't dwelled on Ari's hesitance over him meeting her family the entire time that he was there.

11

Ari pushed her food around her plate, not feeling particularly hungry. While Bjorn had kissed her goodbye, and promised to be waiting for her when she got home, she couldn't ignore the hurt she'd seen in his eyes when she hadn't immediately said he could come with her. Everyone thought that Bjorn was all tough exterior, but she knew better. He actually had one of the kindest hearts she'd ever encountered, and she'd hated leaving him the way she had that morning.

"Ari, are you listening?" Her Mum broke through her brooding and she had to think back quickly to try to remember what they were talking about, but unfortunately, she kept coming up blank.

"Sorry Mum, what did you say?" She asked with a smile, hoping her Mum would forgive her lapse in attention.

"Ari's too busy thinking about a man," Christine teased, causing her Mum's expression to change from one of frustration, to one of shocked excitement.

"Really?"

"I was just teasing," Christine amended quickly, after noticing how uncomfortable Ari looked.

"Is it Kumo? He's got a bit of a reputation, but he's a handsome one, and from a good family," her Mum prattled on, making Ari pull a face of disgust that only Christine saw. She was probably lucky that her Dad and brothers were too interested in their food to be paying any attention to any discussion about Ari's love life.

"No, Mum…" she started, meaning to tell her about Bjorn.

"Craven then? He's a little on the grey side, but with your colouring, the pups will be a beautiful colour!"

"Mum…" Ari tried again, but she could see from the light in her eyes that she wasn't going to stop.

"Oh, and I think one of his sisters might be perfect for Brandon," her brother looked up at the sound of his name, but looked away quickly when he noticed both of his sisters shaking their heads and giving him warning looks.

"Diana, that's enough," her Dad interrupted and Ari shot him a grateful look.

"I only want to know what fox we'll be inviting into our family, George." Ari's heart sunk. Even though her Mum was listing the fox shifters she'd grown up living around, she'd still been secretly hoping that she'd moved past her insistence on Ari mating with another fox. After all, Christine had already done just that. While Ari had never asked her twin if it was a true mating or not, she seemed happy and she'd been blessed with children, so it seemed likely that it was.

"And she'll tell us in her own time," her parents looked at each other with genuine smiles, though Ari knew that it hadn't always been that way. It had taken her Dad years to convince her Mum that she didn't have to wait on him hand and foot, but as that had been what she'd been brought up to believe, and it had been hard work to make her see that she didn't have to act that way. In fact, her Dad's past show of patience and support seemed very similar to the way that Bjorn had waited for her. That thought finally brought a smile to her face, along with a knowing look from Christine.

"Whoever he is, he's a lucky fox," her Mum clapped her hands together.

"Mum…" her smile fell, and she knew that really it was going to have to be now or never.

"Yes, Ari?" She smiled and put a forkful of food in her mouth, chewing slowly as she waited for Ari to continue.

"What if he isn't a fox?" Her Mum's fork clattered against her plate as she dropped it, and even her brothers stopped eating to pay attention. Christine and her Dad both looked interested, but their expressions were nothing like the one on her Mum's face. Christine nodded and gave Ari a small smile, making her wonder just what she knew. Shifter social circles weren't large, and if someone had been talking…well her relationship with Bjorn might not be as secret as she thought it was.

"Well why wouldn't he be? There's plenty of nice fox shifters for you to choose from, it's not like you need to look elsewhere!"

"Diana…" her Dad warned, but it was too late. Tears were welling up in Ari's eyes, spurred on by her Mum's backwards attitude.

"Don't Diana me. It's true."

"So, you won't accept me with someone that isn't a fox?" Ari asked, just about keeping the tears at bay. She chided herself, feeling ridiculous for being so weak. She could hold her own in the courtroom and make other shifters almost quiver in fear in the Council chamber, but when it came to her Mum's prejudice, it was everything she could do to keep it together.

"I don't see why we'd have to," she replied, not even looking at Ari. Christine gestured to get Ari's attention, mouthing words at her in an attempt to get her to leave before she said anything else.

"Mum, did you know that Evan shifted for the first time?" Christine asked, drawing their parent's attention to her litter. Ari pushed back her chair as quietly as she could and fled the room while her Mum was distracted. Though Christine's distraction hadn't worked on their Dad, and she could feel him watching her as she left the room. She knew he was concerned, but given the tears that were threatening to fall, it was probably best that she didn't turn around to reassure him.

12

Bjorn paced back and forth in the living room of Ari's flat, worried despite himself. She'd given him a key and told him to make himself comfortable when they'd left earlier. Yet, while he knew that she was safe and with her family, he just couldn't seem to shake the idea that she needed him.

He sat down at her table, pulling out some notes from one of his cases. If there was no chance of him getting any rest, then he might as well put his time to good use and do some work, at least until she got home. He smirked to himself as he thought about what they'd be doing once she got back; he probably wouldn't get much rest then either.

He grimaced as he read one of his most recent briefs; a wife who thought her husband was cheating on her, but needed proof for a divorce. He hated cases like that, they made him feel like true love wasn't real any more. But today, it also made him thankful that Ari would never have to feel like this woman did. He didn't want to look at another woman, nor did he feel the need to. More than that, he actually couldn't. Even before they'd actually finished the mating process, he'd known that she as the one for him and that was all it took for his interest in other women to fade. Not that he'd ever been overly interested in them anyway; at least, not for anything more than sex. It seemed a little callous, even to him, but after his family had died, he'd known that the only person he'd risk feeling anything for ever again was his mate. If he was lucky enough to find her. Bjorn leaned back in his chair, sighing and pushing a hand over his face. It seemed that work wasn't going to happen, especially if something as disheartening as a cheating husband was making him think of Ari. He was love struck and there was no way to deny it.

He stood up, stretching his arms above his head as he did and decided to investigate Ari's flat a bit more. He hadn't been paying much attention to his surroundings when they'd come back last night, nor when they'd been getting ready to leave that morning; she was far too distracting for that. Just thinking about their morning together, and the night before, had him revved up and ready to go again, which was all very well, but without Ari around, it was a bit of a waste.

The flat was like Ari; modern, functional and with slight hints at femininity that she'd deny if anyone picked up on, but each one made Bjorn smile. The flat was big for a single woman in her thirties, but considering how good Ari was at her job, the luxury it provided wasn't particularly surprising. He knew that she made a lot, probably more than he did, and he knew that she worked hard for every penny, and that wasn't likely to change. Nor did he want it to. Ari loved her job, and it was important to her, and so it was important to him. And if cubs came along and she wanted to keep working, then he'd happily give up his job as a PI. He only did it to keep himself busy as it was. He smiled to himself as he walked into the spare room and saw a bunk bed with plain white sheets. He imagined their children in the room, with his dark eyes and Ari's auburn hair. The mischievous sparkle in their eyes would be all her too, though he hoped they'd be boys; he didn't think he'd be able to deal with the protective urges a girl would bring out in him. Especially if she looked anything like her mother did. He'd read to them every night, play football with them or take them horse riding, though on second thought, there was a chance that the horses wouldn't like them much with their predator shifter side. It probably wouldn't matter to the beasts if they were foxes or bears either. He'd never really considered children before, but his imaginings were filling him with a content feeling that he hadn't felt in years, if ever.

He moved away from the spare room and into another one, this one slightly smaller, and with a tidy desk inside. From the state of it, he doubted that Ari ever used it, which suited him just fine; he could take it over when she asked him to move in full time. There was also a running machine, with a discarded plastic bottle to the side and an iPod plugged in next to it. A grin broke across Bjorn's face; this should sort his restlessness. As a shifter, he needed to regularly burn off the excess energy that he didn't get to use by shifting; one of the perils of modern living. Then again, it was nothing compared to the perils of living in the wild. He pushed aside the heartache that always came with thoughts of his family, and quickly stripped down to his boxers in order to take a run.

Ari heard someone approaching from behind her, but didn't react until her Dad sat down beside her. She'd hidden herself away in the treehouse the two of them had built when she was a little girl. Christine had been more interested in playing with dolls than playing outside, but looking back, Ari appreciated the time she'd spent alone with her Dad. It had enabled her and Christine to develop their own personalities, even if they were twins. Ari pulled her legs up and wrapped her arms around them, as the two of them sat in silence for a few moments.

"She just needs some time."

"I doubt it," she couldn't help the moping tone in her voice.

"She'll get used to it," he put his arm around her and she leaned her head on his shoulder, appreciating the support he always gave, "I mean she'll have to, considering he's your mate and all," he chuckled slightly, though Ari wasn't too sure why.

"I never said that," she countered quickly, trying to recall if she'd even hinted about Bjorn being her mate.

"You didn't have to. I know how important your work is to you, and your seat on the Council. If this man wasn't your mate, then we wouldn't be having this conversation," she didn't know why she was surprised that her Dad knew her so well, he'd always been able to see through her.

"He had the rules changed for me," she admitted quietly, a part of her was still in disbelief over how far Bjorn had gone for her.

"About mated Council members?" He shifted his head so that he was looking at her and she nodded, causing her Dad to smile, "good, you deserve someone like that," he kissed the top of her head.

"He's a lot like you," her Dad chuckled.

"Ah, maybe not someone like that then," but she could hear the smile in his voice. "You know, I think I like him already."

"You would Dad. It's just Mum I'm worried about it."

"Like I said sweetheart, only until she gets used to the idea," he sounded resigned. "It's just part of how she grew up. Her parents were very traditional, and she still has some of those views, even if they're outdated."

"I know," and she did. She'd known enough of her grandparents to know that some of her Mum's more traditional views weren't really her fault. "And she'll be fine with it until we have children. Then we'll be having this conversation all over again when she discovers they're not foxes."

"Do you really think your Mum will love her grandchildren any less just because they're not foxes? Trust me, Ari. She'll love them no matter what they are, whether that's a wolf, tiger or hawk," he smiled reassuringly at her.

"Bears," she whispered, "they'd be bears." That wasn't technically true. There'd only been a handful of mixed shifter matings that Ari knew about, and there didn't seem to be any pattern in which parent the children took after when they shifted. But the idea of her children being bears just seemed right to her. She wondered whether it was the after effects of the night before that had her thinking like that, or if it was some kind of premonition. She pushed the thought away; shifters didn't have premonitions, it wasn't part of their magic.

"See, now we're getting somewhere!" He smiled bigger this time, his true personality showing through now that she was opening up to him. "So, does your bear shifter have a name?"

"Bjorn Hendricks," his eyes widened in surprise.

"The Council member?" Ari bit her lip nervously. Not many people knew the Council's true identities, and her Dad only knew through her, but she imagined that a lot of shifters might see it as a scandal when they learned of Ari and Bjorn's relationship.

"He quit," she added quickly.

"For you?" She nodded, "good."

"He's a good man, Dad."

"I don't doubt that. I didn't raise you to pick a bad one," he pulled her closer to him again.

"I don't think I really had a choice," she sighed, thinking back to the moment she'd first met Bjorn. If she was honest with herself, it was the same moment that she'd known he'd change her life completely; even if she hadn't wanted to admit that at the time.

"Well I'm looking forward to meeting him. Why don't you arrange for the two of us to have a drink tomorrow night? Maybe if he meets me first, he won't be as terrified of your Mum when he meets her," he chuckled at his joke, and a small laugh escaped from Ari too, her dull spirits lifting slightly at the prospect. She had no doubt that after meeting Bjorn, her Dad would talk him up to the rest of her family and they'd see what an amazing man he was too.

"Okay, I think he'd like that," her Dad rose to his feet and offered her his hand. She took it and he pulled her to his feet beside him before enveloping her in a hug.

"Get home safe sweetheart, and don't worry about it. I'll talk to your Mum."

"Thanks, Dad."

"And I look forward to meeting Bjorn tomorrow. Text me about it," he let her go, and jumped deftly down from the tree house, still surprisingly spry for an ageing shifter. Not that anyone would be able to tell he was old enough to have four grown children. Shifters aged slowly, so while he did look older that Ari, he could still pass for his early thirties. She stayed in the tree house a few minutes longer, watching as her Dad disappeared back into the house.

Slowly, she made her way down the ladder and across to where she'd parked her car. It was only when she was sat in her seat and ready to turn the ignition, that she realised she'd asked Bjorn to wait for her at her flat. After that, it was only her increased senses and fast reflexes that allowed her to get home safely.

14

Time had ticked on, and Bjorn had found himself nodding off on the sofa in Ari's living room, despite his desperation to stay awake for when she got back. But the moment he heard the sound of a key in the door, he was alert, anticipation thrumming through his veins. He wasn't even sure what it was he was so excited about, other than the prospect of seeing her again. They'd been sleeping together for months, so it definitely wasn't the novelty of sex with her, though he had to admit, that still came in a close second. Instead, he felt like this night was important to the two of them; almost like it as the first night of something new.

The moment Ari stepped through the door, Bjorn's heart sunk. His excitement wasn't reflected in her face, in fact she looked pale, almost like she was ill. He rushed over to her and wrapped his arms around her without saying a word. She gripped his shirt tight in one fist, her other arm snaking around his back and holding him close. He wasn't sure how long they stood there, still and unmoving, but he felt the moment her emotions changed. She stepped back, a weak smile on her face but her expression seeming more steady to him. She grabbed his hand and tugged him towards her room, but he shook his head.

"Talk to me," he said quietly, knowing that if they didn't talk now, then they probably wouldn't until at least the morning. If at all, knowing Ari.

"It isn't important," she answered and tried to pull him towards the bedroom again. While she could hold her own in the courtroom and when she sat on the Council, he was physically stronger than she was, and didn't budge. He'd never use his strength and size against her, but right now, he could use it to stop her from skating over the expression on her face when she'd opened the door. He cupped her face in his free hand and looked into her eyes, trying to convey all the love and support he could.

"Anything you're feeling is important," she sighed and broke eye contact, causing Bjorn's heart to sink. He'd hoped that she'd tell him what was bothering her.

"It was just something my Mum said," she muttered, but even that felt forced. He waited patiently, hoping that she'd continue on her own. She let go of his hand and slumped down on the sofa. Bjorn followed, taking a seat and opening his arms in the hope that she'd cuddle up to him. Thankfully, she did, resting her head on his shoulder before continuing, "Mum didn't take the news that my mate isn't a fox shifter very well," she admitted. At first, all he could focus on was that her family might have a problem with him, but it soon sunk in that if her Mum hadn't reacted well, then she had to have told them.

"Will she change her mind?" He asked, his voice low and soothing. Or at least, he hoped it was.

"Eventually. Dad wants to meet you though," she perked up a bit at that and he smiled to himself. He'd expected it to take more time for her to accept their relationship and tell other people about it, but it seemed like he'd been wrong.

"Really?" He could hear the excitement in his own voice, but he didn't care. He'd do anything to make her happy.

"Yes. He wants to go for a drink, just the two of you, tomorrow night."

"Does he know I'm a bear?" He asked, cautious of the fact she'd said her Mum didn't approve and wondering if her Dad shared the same opinion.

"Yes, but he didn't have the same upbringing as Mum did. He's always been more open minded. You'll like him, the two of you are alike," she looked up at him, her big pale eyes filled with a mix of pride and love, and he leaned down to kiss her gently.

"I look forward to meeting him," he said honestly after they broke the kiss. She smiled again, looking more like herself than when she'd first got home.

"Can we go to bed?" She asked and he nodded, knowing from the suggestive grin on her face that the conversation was well and truly over; not that he minded now that she'd opened up.

15

Ari finished her final case report and sent it to her boss, knowing
that it was another well fought case. While she hadn't seen anything
in the notes that suggested there was a paranormal behind the crime,
it had been clear to her that the man on trial had been wrongly
accused. Unfortunately, her intuition, and ability to read people better
than most, weren't admissible court evidence. It had been a close call,
but the jury had seen through the prosecutor's case, and Ari had won
again. Except that this time, it didn't bring the same elated feeling as
normal; probably because she was so distracted.

Her thoughts were all over the place and she just couldn't seem to
get them straight. When she thought of Bjorn, her heart raced and
she almost wanted to break into song; not that that would have been
pleasant for anyone around her. But her Mum's reaction was still
bothering her, and with good reason. She wasn't going to leave Bjorn.
In reality, she probably couldn't leave Bjorn. She'd certainly never
heard of mates breaking apart in the past, it just wasn't like marriage.
So, if her Mum wouldn't come around, then Ari would face losing
her family, and that wasn't something that sat comfortably with her
either.

She sighed, shutting down her computer and shrugging on her
coat, hoping that the short walk home would help clear her head.
She'd purposefully bought a flat near her office, but even so, she
enjoyed walking, it was a chance to let the issues of the day slide
away. Of course, before Bjorn had come along, all she'd done when

she'd got home was work more, unless she had a Council meeting. Even after they'd started sleeping together, nine times out of ten she'd just ended up working. Mostly due to her misguided attempt to keep their sex life separate from their actual lives. She'd known from early on that the two of them had been playing with fire, and she'd been even more certain when Kem had come back to the Council room and told them that he was already mated. It was voicing her knowledge that all mates had to do to start the mating process was meet, that made her realise there was no going back. Though even if they weren't mates, Bjorn doing everything he could to have the rules changed would have been enough to convince her.

She smiled to herself, the stress of the case, and of her Mum's biased opinions, slipping away and left her with only good thoughts of two nights ago. And of the night before, when Bjorn had held her as she slept; she didn't think that she'd ever slept so soundly either. There was no doubt left that Bjorn was the one for her.

She climbed the stairs to her flat slowly, relishing the effects of the walk; it'd been a while since she'd shifted and a lot of the energy that shifting required had built up inside her. She idly wondered if Bjorn would mind her shifting in the flat. It was what she normally did, one of the advantages of being a smaller shifter. She'd change and run around, sometimes she even climbed on the furniture if she was feeling particularly mischievous. When she'd been growing up, her Mum had had a strict rule against being on the furniture in fox form, so even though she owned her own furniture now, it still felt like she was breaking the rules.

Thinking about shifting brought up thoughts of Bjorn, and she wondered how he dealt with the need to shift. It was fine for small shifters like her, they could shift inside and not be noticed by the human population, but shifters of Bjorn's size didn't have that luxury. Come to think of it, she didn't even know how big Bjorn's shifted form was. He was some kind of brown bear, whose animal cousin lived near Russia, but she didn't know just how big they grew. Her curiosity piqued, and she started playing with the notion of asking him to shift for her. It seemed like that would be a big step, after all, she'd never shifted in front of anyone that wasn't her family. Or at least, she hadn't in front of anyone that realised she'd shifted; there'd probably been a handful of humans that had seen her in animal form and dismissed it as just another fox.

Her thoughts skidded to a halt as she approached her apartment and found her Mum leaning against the wall, a relieved look on her face when she saw Ari. They looked alike, but her Mum looked slightly older, with dark brown hair instead of auburn; Ari had got that colouring from her Dad.

"Mum," she smiled nervously. She loved her Mum, and didn't want to feel like they were at odds, but she also didn't know what she was here for, which worried Ari slightly.

"Have you had a good day?" She could hear the strain in her Mum's voice as she tried to act casual.

"It was alright thanks," she fit her key into the door, gesturing for her Mum to go in first, selfishly hoping that Bjorn was already out, and they could avoid having whatever confrontation this was in front of him. He already knew that her Mum was judgemental about the whole situation, she didn't want to make his opinion of her any worse. "Would you like a drink?" She dumped her work bag on the side and made her way over to the fridge to pull out the bottle of wine she had chilling in there; no way was she having this conversation without a glass.

"Please," her Mum answered, and Ari poured two glasses, handing the first one to her before taking a drink, relishing the taste as she swallowed it down.

"You okay?" Ari asked, feeling surprisingly calm given the circumstances.

"I've come to apologise," her Mum moved around to perch on one of the seats at the breakfast bar, fiddling with the bottom of her wine glass as she did. Ari waited patiently, not wanting to give her an easy out.

"If you love this man, whoever he is, then I can get past the fact he's not a fox." Ari grimaced despite herself, it wasn't exactly the most glowing thing for her to say.

"Good."

"Ari…"

"What? You want me to just accept your apology despite the fact that you more or less said you wouldn't accept Bjorn? Just because he's not a fox? You know that's not how these things work, Mum. It's not like I have a choice who my mate is!" She half shouted, unable to stop herself.

"Ari, I said I'm sorry," her Mum looked hurt, but Ari's anger was simmering too much to be ignored.

"I know Mum, but you need to understand that this wasn't easy for me. It took me months to accept Bjorn was my mate as it is, and then another couple of months trying to hide it from everyone around us so we didn't lose our Council seats. And then, that man went and had the rules changed so that I could keep mine, giving up his own in the process. He's been patient and kind, and he's strong and fair. Isn't that the kind of man you want for me?" She was getting worked up, and it was all that she could do to keep the tears at bay, but everything she was saying was true. Bjorn had proved himself time and time again to her, but she was the only person that he should have to prove it to. Her Mum opened her mouth to speak, but Ari held her hand up to stop her, "I'm not done. I love him, and he loves me, but you probably don't realise how much your judgement of him hurts me."

"I'm sorry Ari," her Mum sighed, a pained look crossing her face, "it's just that after your father and I, and Christine and Tyrone, I just kind of assumed that your mate would be a fox too, not a..."

"Bear," Ari finished for her, conflicted. She could understand her Mum's reasoning, but that didn't stop her from feeling angry. She also dreaded to think how she would have reacted if she'd been like Kemnebi, and mated with a whole different type of paranormal. She let out a short laugh at the thought, before stopping herself.

"Will you tell me about him?" She asked hesitantly, almost as if she was worried about how Ari would respond. Feeling like a weight had been lifted from her shoulders, Ari began to tell her about Bjorn, a smile spreading over her face as she talked about him. After what felt like an age, her Mum asked to see a picture, making Ari thankful that Bjorn had insisted they take one the other night.

"Here," she handed her Mum her phone. The photo was of the two of them half looking at the camera, unable to completely take their eyes off one another.

"He's handsome, Ari," her Mum gave her a knowing smile and Ari laughed slightly, the wine had helped to loosen the pair of them up, and they now able to talk about Bjorn without the conflict of the past hour.

"He is, and sweet and charming," she sounded so love struck that she almost hated herself for it. Almost, but not quite. It was definitely worth it.

"So, when can I meet him?" Her Mum nervously took a sip of her wine, watching Ari closely to make sure that she hadn't crossed the line.

"I'm not sure, I'm surprised he's not back by now. He's out with Dad tonight."

"He lives here?" She sounded surprised, but not as much as Ari was. They'd only been out in the open for a couple of days, she hadn't even considered that he'd moved in. Yet he had a toothbrush in the bathroom, and shoes on the rack by the door. She didn't mind the idea of him moving in, rather it filled her with a happy glowing feeling that she barely recognised, but they hadn't actually talked about it yet.

"I don't know, I guess so," she shrugged and busied herself with topping up their wine glasses.

"Sounds like you need to talk about it."

"Yes, I think we do. I've liked having him here, I want him to stay," her Mum smiled at her.

"You look like I did when I first met your father," she covered Ari's hand with her own, and the two of them exchanged looks that said everything they needed to; the past was now the past, and her Mum would work hard to accept Bjorn into the family.

16

Bjorn hated to admit it, but he was nervous. Ari had told her that her father was more of a beta male than an alpha one, but that hadn't done anything to stop his worrying. After all, this was the father of the woman he loved. His approval meant a lot to Ari, and so it meant a lot to Bjorn too.

He glanced around the bar, trying to spot the man who held his future in the palm of his hand. He only had Ari's description to go by, but as soon as the red-headed man entered the bar, he knew he was the right one. Bjorn gave a nervous wave and got a smile in return. He studied the man as he walked towards him. It was easy to see the similarities to Ari, it was there in his pale eyes and his auburn hair. Other than that, he didn't look old enough to have a grown daughter, but that was typical of shifters. From what he remembered of his parents, they didn't look old enough to have him either. He was fairly tall, and athletically toned, with an intelligent glint in his eye that betrayed his relation to Ari far more than his appearance did.

"Bjorn I presume?" He held out his hand and Bjorn took it, shaking firmly and successfully hiding his nerves.

"Yes, sir."

"None of this sir nonsense, call me George. I have a feeling that we're going to be in each other's lives for a long time," he smiled and motioned for the bar tender to bring him a beer. They sat there in silence for a few moments. "So, what do you do, Bjorn?"

"I'm a private investigator," George's eyebrows raised in surprise.

"For paranormals?"

"Not necessarily, anyone can hire me," he shrugged. He kept his job more through a necessity to keep busy. Technically, he didn't need the money; he'd been the sole heir to his family, and they'd been beyond rich. But the loneliness that accompanied their deaths still haunted him, and so he'd become a PI. Hunting down cheating spouses and missing people gave him something to focus on.

"And that'll be enough to support my daughter?" This time it was Bjorn's turn to raise a questioning eyebrow. He had a vague idea of how much Ari earned, and he doubted she needed supporting financially. More than that, he couldn't imagine her wanting to be supported financially. It'd go against everything he knew about her.

"I think that Ari can take care of herself, but it certainly won't cost her to have me around," he answered evenly, despite his inner bear having its hackles raised by the challenge. Luckily, his logical side was winning through, especially knowing just how important this meeting was; not just to him, but to Ari too. George chuckled.

"I see that you know my daughter well!" He clapped Bjorn on the back and pride swelled up within him.

"It's hard not to, she's a force of nature," he smiled to himself, thinking of all the little ways Ari made her personality known. Most of those were also the little things he loved about her, even if her need for independence was sure to drive his inner alpha crazy.

"You'd better look after her," George's eyes fixed him with a heavy stare that left no doubt in Bjorn's mind that, despite the fact that George was slighter than he was, if he hurt Ari then he'd be a dead man.

"With every part of my being," he assured him, getting a deferential nod. The two of them moved on to safer topics, and Bjorn learned more about Ari's family. George was clearly proud of all four of his children, and the way he talked about them made Bjorn long for one of his own. All he'd have to do was convince Ari to have one too, and that wasn't something he was quite so sure of.

"I think it's time to go," George checked his watch, making Bjorn check the time on his phone, and he was surprised to see that three hours had passed. He was also surprised to see a message from Ari telling him that her Mum was at their place. She'd even used the word 'theirs' in her text, making him beam.

"Your wife seems to be at Ari's apartment, I don't have a car with me, but it's not far," he belatedly realised that George probably knew where Ari lived, but the older man nodded anyway and let it slip by. The two of them left the bar and made the short walk back to Ari's flat in comfortable silence.

The sight that greeted the two of them when they arrived there had them both shell shocked for a few moments. It appeared as though Ari and her mother were both drunk, their giggles sounding loud even out in the hallway. The worst of it was that shifters couldn't get drunk unless they wanted to, making Bjorn wonder what the hell had been going on.

"Ari?" He asked, putting more questioning into his voice than he should, but all it did was cause Ari to giggle louder.

"Oh, he's even more handsome in real life!" Her mother ogled him, giggling along with Ari.

"Isn't he?"

"I don't know how you resisted him for so long," she winked, and Bjorn looked away, not quite knowing what to do with himself.

"Come on, Diana. Let's get you home," George went up to his wife and helped her up to her feet.

"Don't worry Georgy, you're handsome too," she kissed him, and it took George a moment to respond, though he pulled back quickly, clearly uncomfortable with her display of affection in front of their daughter.

"Here," in an effort to avoid watching, Bjorn had gone over to the tap in the kitchen and poured a glass of water, handing it to George to give to his wife. He took it with a grateful smile, and Diana drunk slowly under his watch.

"Thanks, I'd better get her home. Good to meet you, Bjorn. Night, sweetheart," he called the last bit to Ari, who was still giggling on the sofa. The two of them began to make their way over to the door, with Diana staggering slightly and George supporting her weight.

"Night, Dad! Night, Mum!" Bjorn padded over to her and sunk down onto the sofa. Ari immediately crawled onto his lap and straddled him, causing Bjorn to look up sharply and breathe a sigh of relief when he saw that her parents had left straight after she'd called goodnight.

"I take it she's come around," he asked, curious as to what had gone on between the two of them.

"Mmmm," Ari answered, kissing his neck and running one of her hands up inside his shirt.

"Ari..." he warned and she looked up, her big pale eyes surprisingly clear, given how out of it she'd seemed only minutes ago.

"Yes," she answered throatily, the sound going straight to Bjorn's groin, something he wasn't able to hide given her position on top of him.

"You've drunk too much for this."

"Have I?" Her eyes sparkle, "I've only had a few glasses of wine. I was just caught in the moment." He wasn't convinced, but at that moment she began grinding against him, and his ability to think rationally flew out the window.

"Ari…" he repeated.

"Fine," she huffed, rising to her feet, the coy smile he loved so much still on her face. "You show me yours and I'll show you mine," he gave her a confused look, not quite sure what she was on about. If it was sex, then they'd been heading there anyway, despite his better judgement. If not, then he really had no clue.

They no longer touched, and a pang of longing went through Bjorn even though she was standing mere feet in front of him. He may have realised that they were mates months ago, but he'd never expected it to affect him quite as much as it did.

Slowly, she unbuttoned her silk shirt, letting it fall to the floor in a messy pile. The moment that her suit skirt followed, Bjorn made to move towards her, but a shake of Ari's head, and the mischievous look in her eye, stopped him. A low growl rumbled through his chest at the sight of her naked in front of him. But he didn't move.

Her expression changed fleetingly, and a moment later, a russet coloured fox stood in her place. Her words finally making sense to Bjorn. He took a moment to admire her. She was a little bigger than a normal fox, but not noticeably so, and she'd more than likely go unnoticed by a human. Her fur looked soft, and he yearned to touch it, before remembering that she was his mate, and that she wouldn't just let him, but would likely encourage it. She cocked her head at him and he reached forward, his hand shaking with inexplicable nerves.

Reverently, he stroked her head, enjoying the silky soft feel of her fur against his hand. She leant her head into his touch, her eyes closing in appreciation and soft yips came from her, letting him know that he was doing the right thing.

"You're beautiful, Ari," he wasn't sure why he whispered, but he did. Her eyes flickered open in a surprisingly human movement, and she fixed him with her shrewd gaze, now completely devoid of the effects of the wine she'd drunk; shifting could do wonders when it came to things like that.

She nudged him, taking on an impatient air despite her current shape. It took him a moment to realise what she was after, but the moment he did, he stood and began to unbutton his jeans, all but ripping them off along with the rest of his clothing. He concentrated on the image of his bear, or at least what he thought his bear looked like; he'd never actually seen it, even in a reflection. In mere seconds, he'd shifted, his form taking up most of Ari's living room.

She studied him for a moment, before shifting back into human form; completely naked, with her auburn hair ruffled gloriously. He dwarfed her in size, but that didn't phase her and she ran her hands through his thick brown fur.

"So are you," she kissed the top of his head, causing a warm, fuzzy feeling go through Bjorn, and without even thinking about it, he shifted back and pulled her to him with a searing kiss. A kiss that felt so right that he wondered how he'd lived without her up until now.

Ari's hands roamed over his chest, raking against his skin with her fingernails and making Bjorn's breath shorten. His hands on her hips, he guided her movements, pulling the two of them back down onto the sofa. She sank down on him, not wasting any time, her head tilting back as he entered her in one swift move. Bjorn tried to focus on anything other than the feel of her around him in an effort to stop him finishing too soon.

The two of them moved against one another, incapable of anything more than moaning and grunting each other's names. It didn't take long for the pleasure to mount within Bjorn. He thrust his hips more furiously, and pulled Ari's face to his, kissing her with unrestrained passion. Ari broke the kiss and threw her head back once more, letting out a long moan. He felt her pulse around him, breaking his concentration and the two of them finished in unison, collapsing into a sweaty heap on the sofa, satisfied and content.

17

2 years later…

Ari watched as Bjorn made his way to her, a drink in each hand and a smile on his face. He kissed her softly and handed her one of the glasses, before sitting down next to her. He pulled her to him, one arm around her shoulders, and the other hand resting on her rounded stomach. It had taken her a couple of years to be ready to have a family, despite the guilt she'd felt, knowing how desperate Bjorn had been for children. But she had to admit that now she was pregnant, she felt completely different, and couldn't wait to become a Mum.

"You sure you're ready for this?" He asked softly enough that her family couldn't hear. They were at her parents for Christmas dinner, along with Christine and her family.

"It's a bit late for that now," she teased him.

"Well yes, but…"

"Bjorn, we talked about this. I'm ready for a family, because that family is with you," she touched his cheek gently and he turned to kiss her palm, sending a tingly feeling through her and making her wish that they were alone.

"And you're okay with giving up work?" She knew that he was particularly worried about her giving it up, but she'd thought it through and decided it would be the best way to go. She'd kept her seat on the Council though, and would for as long as she could.

"I'm fine with it for now. It's not like we need the money, and being there for the kids is going to be the most important thing," she hadn't discovered just how much money Bjorn had until they started talking about kids and if they could afford them. Between her own savings, Bjorn's inheritance and his income from his PI work, they were more than set and their kids would never lack for anything. Not that she thought they would, there was no way that could happen with Bjorn as a father.

"But in the future…"

"In the future I might go back to work, but in the future the kids will be at school and things may have changed."

"Okay," he kissed the top of her head, but didn't stay any longer as her Dad had called him over to help him with dessert. It'd always been that way, her Mum cooked dinner, and her Dad did dessert. It was something he now liked to share with his two son-in-laws. Most likely cause her brothers just weren't interested in the slightest.

She watched as he chatted with her Dad, and with Christine's kids, and couldn't wait for the day that she'd get to see Bjorn with their own. She touched her stomach, feeling one of the twins kicking, and smiled; that day was coming soon, and when it did, she suspected that it would be the happiest day of her life.

ABOUT THE AUTHOR

I like to write whichever weird and wonderful tale comes into my head, which makes identifying the genre difficult even for me! My first series, Alventia, are novellas centred around Keira, aka Sleeping Beauty, and her Prince Philip, along with their allies Hansel and Gretel. It's a tale that very much told itself as I started to write it!

While I'm not writing, I work in Catering and am also an Assistant Brownie Guide Leader in the Midlands (UK). I like to bake and I love to read, and like with my writing, I read an eclectic mix of genres, and love every minute of it!

Also by Laura Greenwood

Paranormal Council (Paranormal Romance)
The Dryad's Pawprint
The Vixen's Bark
The Necromancer's Prey (Coming Soon!)

Alventia Series (Fantasy)
Betrayed (Mailing List Exclusive)
Awakening
Cloaked

Curtain Call (NA Romance)
What Lies Beneath the Mask
You Know I Do

Anthologies
Touched by Shadow, Caressed by Light
The Newcomer: Twelve Sci-Fi Short Stories
Christmas in Love

Stand Alone
By Any Other Name: A Retelling of Romeo & Juliet (Paranormal)

18132687R00045

Printed in Poland
by Amazon Fulfillment
Poland Sp. z o.o., Wrocław